Harry Potter Spells, Facts and Fantastic Beasts

The Ultimate Guide Book of Spells, Secret Trivia
and Fantastic Beasts for Wizards and Witches

By: William Gray

Table of content

Chapter One---
-SpellBook

Introduction

An unruly wizard (must not be named, of course) is at it again. This time, all spell books at Hogwarts are missing. The ministry has no clue how this callous intruder got hold of them, including the sacred copies at Gringotts Wizarding Bank. But! Justice shall prevail, and we must replace every single one of the lost spells. Join me as we rewrite a new spellbook and incantations.

In a nutshell, this magical spellbook is a completion of all magical powers expressed in Harry potter. Keeping in mind the various faculties of magic spells, this book has been divided into (charms, Healing spells, counter-spells, transfiguration spells, counterspells, hexes, jinxes and curses). We hope the sorting hat leads you right to the particular spells you need and with that determine what type of witch or wizard you are.

Section 1 Charms

Charms are spells that alter an object, yet retains the essential attributes/nature of the objects. They target other wizard's capabilities and abilities. Wizards over the years have used charms of various forms to manipulate objects and bend nature to their will. The charms class as taught by professor Flitwick bears spells such as the summoning, banishing, and aviation spells. Harry, Ron, and Hermione were dedicated students of the charms class. Often taking advantage of common curses such as Wingardium Laviosa and Alohomora to get out of trouble.

However, witches notably Mrs. Longbottom, who also is Neville's grandmother, consider Charms to be a "soft option" even at N.E.W.T year level. For the few students opportuned to study charms, absolute care must be taken; even harry potter encountered great difficulty with some charms especially the summoning charm.

Accio

Summoning Charm. This charm summons an object to the caster, potentially over a significant distance.

1.Accio /ˈæki.oʊ/ ak-ee-oh (Summoning Charm) .

First used by our dear harry at the Triwizard tournament to summon his firebolt broomstick, the Accio spell is a summoning charm useful when the spell caster wished to bring an object to him/herself. Who didn't feel relieved when Harry smartly used the Accio spell to retrieve the Triwizard cup when dueling with Lord Voldemort?

The Accio charm is one of the most commonly known charms in the Wizarding world. Used over a dozen times by wizards in the ministry, the spell is a vital tool during wars and duels within and outside the walls of Hogwarts. As student's this spell is unavoidably taught in the 4th year and in the 5th years at Hogwarts right before the O.W.Ls examinations.

Effects and casting

The charm cannot be used on living objects, although there is a way around this. Simply cast it on something they wear or are on, and it works just perfectly. Secondly, the charm doesn't work on large fixated objects such as mountains and buildings. Special care, however, must be taken while using the summoning spell on humans to avoid injuries as it travels with the speed of light.

Aguamenti

This Charm Creates a gush of water from the tip of the spell caster's wand

2.Aguamenti / ˌɑːgwəˈmɛnti/ ah-gwə-men-tee

Seamus Finnigan's Aguamenti Charm couldn't have been handier when he had a duel with Professor Flitwick. The Agumenti spell produces jets of water from one's wand. The propulsion and speed of the water are dependent on the movement of the wand. Harry and Hagrid used the Aguamenti spell to put out the fire that started in Hagrid's Hut.

The water making spell doubles as a charm and a conjuration, which is an advanced form of transfiguration. Most witches and wizards believe the water spell is a counter-spell to the fire-making spell. However, for advanced fire-making spells such as Fendfyre, the Aguamenti is totally unhelpful as such fires are cursed flames conjured by dark magic.

Effects *and casting*

The casting wand movement for the Aguamenti spell involves a smooth wave movement from right to left. Also, for young wizards, this spell is only taught in the sixth year at Hogwarts.

Alohomora

Unlocking Charm: This charm is used to unlock and open doors. It is possible to curse a door to counteract the spell.

3.Alohomora / əˌloʊhəˈmɔərə/ ə-loh-hə-mohr-ə (Unlocking Charm)

Used by magicians to open doors and hidden treasures. First used by the dark lord (Voldemort) to break into Potter's house and by Miss Granger to unlock the to open a forbidden entrance on the Third-floor corridor of Hogwarts Castle. Alohomora spell allows unlocking anything locked. Not only doors or windows, but it can also unlock chests and other objects. The Alohomora spell is effective against the things locked with Colloportus, which is locking spell.

The Alohomora has an Anti-spell, which in this case, counteracts the effect of the spell. If a magical lock was placed on a door, the Anti-Alohomora spell could break it.

Effects *and casting*

The Alohomora spell originated from west Africa, and means "Friend of the thefts" I the native language, because of its popularity among magically savvy thieves. Also, there is a powerful version of the spell, capable of breaking through fortified places called the Alohomora Duo.

4.Aparecium / ˌæpəˈriːsi.əm/ ap-ə-ree-see-əm: *Reveals invisible ink*

It is a charm that turns all hidden text, writing's and markings visible. With it, no secret is left hidden even with an invisible ink or a concealing charm.

Rumors have it that the Horcrux spell is the only spell that can block the power of the Aparecium.

Effects

The Aparecium charm is used by simply tapping on a book or parchment with your wand, and any hidden message will be revealed. The wand moment is a simultaneous combination of a twirl and a stroke on the parchment you wish to reveal.

5.Piertotum Locomotor (peer-TOH-tuhm loh-kuh-MOH-tor): *Animates target*

Who amongst us didn't heave a sigh of hope when Professor Minerva McGonagall cast this spell during the second wizarding war, order of the phoenix. The excited professor couldn't help but confess that she's always wanted to use this enchanting spell. The piertotum locomotor spell is an incantation for a charm used in bringing to life inanimate artifacts.

Effects

This spell works best on gargoyles and stone artifacts, hence animating them and bending them to the caster's will. The Latin translation thus is "I move thee forth, all dutiful" wand movement is Hold wand aloft (when animating multiple things) or Point wand at target (when animating individual target).

6.Expecto Patronum (ex-PEK-toh pa-TRO-num) *Creates a Patronus*

Also known as the most used spell in harry potter. It is the most famous and the most dominant defensive charms known to wizard world. No other charm can produce the kind of protection a Patronus evokes in defense against dark spirits and creatures. It is an immensely complicated and tough spell to invoke because it requires you focus on a positive memory in the presence of fright an action not many witches and wizards find very easy to do. The vast majority of witches and wizards are unable to produce any form of Patronus, and to create even an intangible one is generally considered a mark of superior magical ability. Rubeus Hagrid is an example of a wizard that cannot conjure any form of Patronus, as the charm is too difficult for him.

The Lethifold (also known as the Living Shroud) is a carnivorous and highly dangerous magical beast. Just like dementors, the only known charm capable of warding off these demonic creatures is the Patronus charm.

Effects

There are two types of Patronus: first the corporeal Patronus which means a Patronus of a peculiar shape of an object or animal likened to the imagination of the caster very effective in protecting against dementors.

The second is the incorporeal Patronus which has no shape and offers no protection against dementor as much as the corporeal Patronus. However, some wizards like Remus Lupin choose to cast incorporeal Patronuses to hide their identity.

The wand movement for casting aPatronuss charm is a circular twirl that gives off a silver light thus giving off a spirit guardian known as a Patronus. In harry potter. Also, remember that only the pure of heart can produce a Patronus. Mostly when skilled witches and wizards cast a Patronus it takes the form of their favorite animal as an indicator of obsession or eccentricity.

Various Wizards and Their Patronuses

Harry Potter
o Harry's patronus is a stag, same as James, hi, father.
Minerva McGonagall
o A cat as expected
Severus Snape
o A Doe the the same as Lily potter.
Nymphadora Tonks
o Nymph has two Patronus. One a wolf anjackrabbitbit. Her initial Patronus was Jackrabbit but inadvertently changed to a wolf due to her love for Remus who's patronus is a wolf as well.
Albus Dumbledore
o The most powerful wizard and principal of Hogwarts assumed no other form than that which he's always been known for, a Phoenix.
Hermione Granger
o an otter.
Remus Lupin
o Remus Patronus is Wolf, identical to his nature as a werewolf.
Luna Lovegood
o Ever pure and innocent just as the hare which was her patronus

7.Duro (DYOO-ROH) *Turns an item to stone*

This charm is also known as the Hardening charm. Used to turn objects into stone.

The hardening spell originated from ancient Portugal and Spain. It means "I stiffen" or "I harden."

Effects

The hardening charm doubles as both a charm and a transfiguration spell. Taught in the third year at Hogwarts by Professor Minerva McGonagall. The wand movement is a letter D. famous Practitioners include; Hermione Granger and Miner McGonagall.

8.Engorgio (en-GOR-gee-oh) *Makes an item larger, as in swollen*

The Engorgio spell is handy for turning objects larger than they ordinarily are. Although helpful in some cases, it is considered an extremely dangerous charm. Because oftentimes the resulting effect cannot be controlled by the wizard. wizards who practice this charm must learn the counter-charm, which is the Reducio spell.

Ron Weasley initially thought that Rubeus Hagrid might have gotten in the way of a bad Engorgement Charm when he was young, not realizing that he was half-giant.

Effects

The engorgio spell is cast by making a "V" shape with a wand. It is also known as the Growing charm in the magical world. It can also serve as a counter-spell to the Reducio spell, which shrinks objects down from their original size.

It appears as a circle of icy blue light coming forth from the tip of the wand, much like a torch. Turning anything within this circle exponentially bigger than usual bouncing and shivering as it grows.

A point to note for young practicing wizards is that the spells won't grow an object beyond a specific limit. Which goes to say that continuous casting of the spell on a particular object might cause it to explode. This spell is taught in the second year of Hogwarts.

Geminio

This charm creates a duplicate of an item (a twin, as in the zodiacal sign Gemini).

9.Geminio (juh-MIN-ee-oh)

The Germinio spell is both a charm and a curse used to create duplicates of objects. It is used mostly to create confusion when cloaking an original item from unwanted hands. As a curse, it is known as the Gemino cursed used to curse an object into repeatedly multiplying when touched. Hermione used this spell to create an exact replica of the locket stolen from Dolores Umbridge, an act which had saved them from the owner noticing that her actual property had been stolen.

Effects

Most wizards wonder if the doubling copy of an Objected created through the Geminio spell holds the same value as the original copy as most times, the two objects are impossible to tell apart. One is identical to the other. Studies show that over time the copy object rots and gets worn out faster than the original object. For this reason, the replicas created from this spell hold no value against the original object.

It is still unknown if the spell can duplicate living creatures and human beings as well as magical objects which have magical properties, and if so, do they retain their magical properties. The Geminio charm does not affect souls and fundamental entities including metaphysical entities. This is why when Hermione Granger cast this spell on the Slytherin's locket the resulting locket lacked all the powers of the original thus prompting the death of the dark lord Voldemort during the battle at Hogwarts.

An important note to take into consideration is that the Geminio spell can only be stopped by the counter-curse from the original caster. If, however, the original incantation was not correctly concluded by the caster the multiplication continues unstoppable and Irreversible. This indefinite replication property can be done deliberately as a security measure, where it is known as the Gemino Curse.

10.Portus (POR-tus)

Portus

This Charm turns any item into a Portkey, which can then be used to transport a person or persons to another location.

Portus is the incantation of a spell used in creating Portkeys. Portkeys are magical portals used in transporting witches and wizards from one realm/location to another. This a restricted form of magic, regulated by the ministry of magic, which is solely responsible for the creation of portkeys. The usage of this spell is limited outside the jurisdiction of the ministry.

Effect

The work Portkey originated from the Latin word " Portare" which means "to carry." Once this spell is cast on an object, the object glows with blue light, as is common with the light given off by a portkey. However this glow is often short-lived as the object now a portkey returns back to its normal state.

11.Reparo (reh-PAH-ROH): *Repairs broken items*

According to the standard book of spells, the Reparo charm is repair objects to their wholesome original state. Also known as "the Mending charm" it is the handiest spell in the wizarding world where most incantation results in the destruction of objects. This incredibly useful and practical charm was invented by Orabella Nuttley in 1754. Hermoine cast this spell to repair Harry's damages eyeglasses.

Effects

It is useful in repairing damages on a wide range of materials and especially inanimate objects with exception to damages caused by powerful spells such as the FiendFyre.

It is important not to use this spell on humans or animals in a bid to heal wounds, this could cause severe scarring. There numerous healing spells for that purpose.

While a properly cast Mending Charm was generally enough to fix an object, it seems less experienced casters might not succeed in returning liquids to broken containers.

This spell cannot mend damages incurred on a powerful magical object such as the vanishing cabinet and broken wands. Although the charm can repair the physical form of a wand, it, however, cannot restore it to its magical state. Only the Elder wand can successfully repair a damaged wand.

Section II Healing Spells

Healing spells are specific spells used to magically alter the physical wellbeing of a living entity. It comes within a branch of magic known as healing magic. There are various spells dedicated to this branch of magic, and they all have variety of Effects . Some healing period works with a combination of potions, and there are broad categories of potions dedicated to healing purposes as well. When a witch or a wizard is dedicated to this area of magic, they are referred to as healers and Mediwizards. Madame Pomfrey is the mediwarzard in charge of the Hogwarts hospital wing. Other notable healers encountered by harry potter include Molly Wesley, Hermione Granger, Severus snape, Remus lupin, and Miriam Strout.

Of the seven known categories of a spell, the Healing spells are distinguished as peaceful and helpful. Popular potions known to aid the effective use of a healing spell includes; Mandrake juice, skele gro, pepperup tonic, Murtlap Essence, Wolfsbane Potion, Mixture of powdered silver and dittany, Sleeping Draught, Calming Draught, Wiggenweld Potion, Poison Antidotes, Dr Ubbly's Oblivious Unction, Wideye or Awakening Potion and Burn-healing paste.

1.Anapneo (ah-NAP-nee-oh): *spell to clear the throat of a choking victim.*

Culled from the Greek word Anapneo (αναπνέω) which means "I breathe." In the half-blood prince, we could see the use of the Anapneo spell when Horace Slughorn used the spell to help poor chocking Marcus Belby, who got himself chocking why eating. Anapneo is the healing spell whose incantation cleared the target's airway by vanishing whatever the target was choking on.

Effects and casting

There are no adverse Effects of the Anapneo spell. However, healers advise the use of caution when waving the want to avoid plucking out someone's eye in the process.

2.Brackium Emendo (BRAH-kee-um eh-MEN-doh) /Ossio Dispersimus: *heals brachial bones*

Contrary to the mess Gilderoy Lockhart made with this spell, it is a pretty effective spell used for fixing broken bones. Used only once in harry potter when harry fell off his broomstick during Quiddich game. However, the naïve professor made improper use of the spell cast on young Harry's hand and thus proceeded to magically remove all bones instead.

Effects and casting

The Brackium Emendo spell can only be used once on a person, a repeat of the cast spell will cause instant paralysis. Hence witches/wizards who perform this spell undergo years of practice to perfect and do it accurately. No wonder professor Lockhart made a mess of it.

The potion Skele-Gro can be used to restore damages caused by the improper use of the Brackium Emendo. The Skele-gro potion is used to magically regrow skeletal parts.

3.Episkey (eh-PIS-kee): *Heals minor injuries*

Episkey is a useful spell for healing minor injuries. The incantation is often seen as a first-aid tool in the Wizarding world.

Effects and casting

The Episkey spell could prompt a sudden change in body temperature to anyone the incantation was used on. Commonly used to fix a broken nose, toes, or split lips.

4.Ferula (fer-ROOL-lah): *Bandaging Charm*

Ferula is a charm used to bandage and splint broken bones. In the third year of Hogwarts (Prisoner of Azkaban), Lupin uses the spell to strap up Ron's leg, as he would instead let Madam Pomfrey mend it.

Effects and casting

The ferula is a healing charm, conjured when Mediwizards and healers wish to apply bandages to a patient's wound. The bandages are also deemed to have healing powers also. To cast a Ferula, simply point and tap the target.

5.Reparifors (re-PAR-i-fors): *Heals minor magically induced ailments*

Reparifors is an incantation of a healing charm used Heals minor magically induced ailments. These injuries include paralysis and poisoning. Culled from Latin, and means "chance, luck, fortune."

Effects and casting

The spell, much like most healing spells, gives off a purple glow when cat. It may also be used as an incantation for transfiguration.

6.Vulnera Sanentur *(VUL-ner-ahsah-NEN-tour)*

The Vulnera Sanentur doubles as both a healing spell and a counter-spell. Created by Professor Severus Snape, the spell is known to knit wounds and prevent loss of excess blood.

The song-like magic of a healing spell and counter-curse to the Sectumsempra Spell, both of which were invented by Professor Severus Snape under his alias of "Half-Blood Prince." In this particular incident, "Snape knelt over Malfoy, drew his

14

wand, and traced it over the deep wounds Harry's curse had made, muttering an incantation that sounded almost like song. The flow of blood seemed to ease; Snape wiped the residue from Malfoy's face and repeated his spell. Now the wounds seemed to be knitting".

Effects and casting

The Vulnera Sanentur curse must be repeated thrice for it to be cast. The Wand movement is to trace wand over wounds or Poke wound with a wand. Unfortunately, Body parts that had been completely removed with Sectumsempra could not be restored even using this spell.

Section III
Transfiguration
Spells

Transfiguration spells are spells used to alter the appearance of the target. They change the physical morphology of an object. It is a branch of magic that focuses on the alteration of the form or appearance of an object, through the modification of the object's molecular structure. It is the only form of spell that has no barrier to which its Effects can go; that is, it works on all objects upon which it is cast.

Transfiguration, however, is a complicated branch of magic. It requires hard work and a scientific approach unlike other forms of magic. A practicing witch or wizard must adhere strictly to all instructions for it to be success.

There are various types of transfiguration spells, each with its specific spell. Transformation (altering

The physical features of targets), Switching, Vanishment, Conjuration (transfigures objects from thin air), and Untransfiguration.

There are several factors a wizard must take into account when carrying out Transfiguration spells. The intended transformation is directly influenced by body weight, viciousness , wand power , concentration, and a fifth unknown variable Here are some transfiguration spells. Transfiguration is taught from the first years of study at Hogwarts.

1.Lapifors (LAP-i-fors): *transforms small objects into rabbits.*

The Lapifors spell is a transfiguration spell that transforms a little object into a rabbit. Commonly used in circus and magical exhibitions as a means of entertainment. Often it is practiced on small statues, little animals such as salamanders and cats. It can also work on humans, but it hasn't been generally tested. Witches and wizards who practice the Lapifors spell are mostly circus magicians, theater entertainers, and expressional artists.

Effects and casting

A rabbit produced off the spell is subject to the caster's command. The caster has full control of whatever the rabbit does, including the direction of movement. This spell is learned in the third year at Hogwarts school of witchcraft and wizardry under the tutelage of Professor Minerva McGonagall dean of transfiguration studies.

Orchideous

This charm makes a bouquet of flowers appear out of the tip of the caster's wand

2.Orchideous (or-KID-ee-us)

Orchedous is an ornamental spell used by magical florists and decorators to conjure flowers from the tip of their wand. According to magical florist Garrick Ollivander, "Orchedous is more of an incantation than a spell of transfiguration. It is classified under the conjuration type of transfiguration.

Effect

In the fourth year of Hogwarts, Minerva McGonagall takes students through the intricacies of the Orchideous spell. The wand movement is a gentle circular movement while muttering the spell, it gives off a pink glow from a wand.

3.Avifors (AH-vi-fors): *Turns things into birds*

The Avifors spell is a transfiguration spell as well as a bird conjuring charm, known to transform things into birds. Taught by the head of the transfiguration class Professor Minerva McGonagall at Hogwarts, young wizards are expected to practice with small objects such as toys and statues. The essence of the Avifors spell is to create a temporary animal of amusement.

According to Miranda Goshawk, transfiguration is one of the most challenging magic to practice, because it involves the transformation of something inanimate to a living, moving creature.

Effects

It is one of the most complicated transfigurations spells thus, only few in the magical realms have been able to master and perfect it. The Avifors Spell was learned during first year and revised in second year Transfiguration class with Professor McGonagall and was included in The Standard Book of Spells, Grade 2, by Miranda Goshawk. The wand movement to cast the Avifor spell is a sideways figure eight. Known practitioners of this spell include Minerva McGonagall, harry potter, Ron Weasley, and Hermione Granger.

4.Vera Verto (vair-uh VAIR-toh): *Transforms animals into water goblets!*

Known as Professor McGonagall's favorite spell. The Vera Verto spell is the incantation of a transfiguration spell used in transforming animals into water goblets.
"Could I have your attention, please? Right, now, today, we will be transforming animals into water goblets. Like so. One, two, three. Vera Verto."

—Professor McGonagall to her second years

It is more of an ornamental incantation used by circus magicians to create amusement. Animals susceptible to this spell are specifically aves, rodents, and felines. A failed attempt is somewhat disastrous as you could be left with a half-animal/ half glass goblet as with the case of Ron Weasley.

Effects

A highly intricate spell to perform, every action from incantation to wand movement must be carried out accordingly. The hand movement is to tap the wand three times on the intended animal while chanting Vera Verto. Once rightly done, a jet of nearly indiscernible bright mist will jet off from the wand a crackling, whining noise unto the animal, simultaneously turning it into a glass goblet. If performed incorrectly the light produced is green instead, and there is a partial transformation of the animal. Known practitioners include Minerva McGonagall and Jacob Sibling.

Section IV Counter-Spells

Counterspells are specific spells that target and nullify the effect of target spells. Could also mean a type of spell where the primary effect is to inhibit, remove, or negate the Effects of another spell. A countered spell is entirely negated and the energy carried within in sent back or vanishes. This might cause a rebound effect on the caster or objects upon which it was intended or previously cast.

Counterspells are used very often to counter the effect of dark magic. In harry potter, this protective spell was used severally by practising witches and wizards, students and even magical creatures. For example, lily potter's sacrificial death instantly let out sacrificial protection against the dark lord's killing curse, an event which later led to the downfall of Lord Voldemort and leaving young harry with a scar.

1.Finite Incantatem (fi-NEE-tay in-can-TAH-tem): *counters all spell Effects*

Known as the ultimate counter-spell. The Finite Incantatem spell is a general counterspell that counters a wide range of target spells. It is a handy tool in reversing minor Jinxes, hexes and curses during magical duels. It is also used to protect homes from offensive enchantments. This counter-spell is taught in the second year charms class of Hogwarts School of witchcraft and wizardry.

Considered one of the most counter-spell against dark spells. For instance the Protego Diabolica fire can be quenched if a strong witch or wizard casts a Finite incantantem against it as seen when Gellert Grindelwald cast the spell to separate his allies from foes. In a nutshell the finite incantation is a handy tool for any witch or wizard.

Effects

The spell terminates all spell effect upon chanting its incantation. It gives off a red light when cast.

2.Meteolojinx Recanto (mee-tee-OH-loh-jinks reh-KAN-toh):
to counter atmospheric changing spells

The Meteolojinx Recanto is a chant to a counter-charm that nullifies the Effects caused by weather-modifying charms such as the atmospheric charm. The incantation 'meteo' is derived from the word meteorology which is the science of the atmosphere and weather which originates from the Greek word metéōron. 'Recanto' itself is culled from the Latin word 'recantare' which means to withdraw.

This spell proved useful in reversing the effect of the weather spell cast by the dark lord when he took control over the ministry of magic. His spell caused rain to rain in offices, thus destroying lots of vital information.

Effects

It causes weather Effects caused by incantations to cease. The wand movement is a pointed stroke while muttering the incantation. It doesn't give off any light when cast unlike other counter-spells.

3.Surgito (SUR-jee-toh): *Removes enchantments*

Surgito is the incantation of the enchantment removal counter-charm. Originally from ancient Rome, the spell has been used for ages to unbind people from magical enchantment such as love spells and confusion charms. Surgito is a Latin word in

21

the imperative form meaning "you/he/she shall arise, or get up". The word surge means "I arise "in conversational Latin. Thus the spell can be likened to waking up from a confused, dreamlike state.

Counters enchantments and love spells. Appeared mostly in fantastic beasts; the crimes of Grindelwald.

4.Reverte (ree-VUHR-tay): *reveres damaged objects to their original state.*

Reverte is counter-charm used in reversing objects to their original state. It acts like a rewind of scenes in a movie. Just like most counter-spells, the Reverte spell originated from ancient Rome. In Latin, the word Reverte means "to return" or 'turn back". It is often likened with another counterspell "Offero" which perform a specific counteraction.

5.Liberacorpus (lib-er-ah-COR-pus): *counters the jinx Levicorpus*

Created by professor Severus snape, little wonder this same counter-spell ended up saving him when James potter reversed the levicorpus spell he cast on him earlier on lily's request. Levicorpus is the incantation of a jinx. The spell, causes the victim to be hoisted into the air by their ankle; the Liberacorpus is the only known counter-spell to reverse the effect of this dark jinx.

Unaware by students during his era, this jinx and counter-jinx were invented by Severus Snape and recorded under his pseudonym the "Half-Blood Prince" during his time as a student at Hogwarts School of Witchcraft and Wizardry.

Harry used the Liberacorpus counter-spell to counteract the effect of the levicorpus he accidentally cast on Ron.

Although created at a very tender age by Severus snape as a form of amusement and fun amongst students, both spell and counter-spell are regarded as advanced dark magic in the wizarding world. Cast by jerking the wand upwards, the spell has no light or aura attached with it.

6. Vipera Evanesca (vee-PARE-uh eh-vuh-NES-kuh): *vanishing of snakes*

For what it's worth, Snape deserved to be the defence against dark arts teacher, for the most part of his life, he invented most important counter-spell against vicious dark spells.

The snake vanishing spell is a transfiguration spell as well as counter-spell that vanishes magically conjured snakes. This spell was demonstrated when Draco Malfoy conjured a vicious spell during the duel with harry potter in the chambers of secrets, an incident which leads to the discovery of Harry's parseltongue abilities. Snape destroyed and vanished the serpent using the Vipera Evanesca spell.

The Vipera Evanesca spell is specific to snakes conjured from dark magic. The wand movement is a wave from the wand in the form of a snake while chanting the spell. If properly cast, the snake lights up in flames giving off black smoke.

7. Emancipare (eh-man-ci-PAR-eh): *Releases bindings*

For any binding spell, be it dark magic or ordinary spell. The Emancipare spell is the only known spell to release the effect of binding spells. The term Emancipare is an incantation to a counter-charm that can release people from binding spells. It is a counter-spell to most provocative target spells such as Fulgari, Brachiabindo and Incarcerous spell. Known wizards who have cast this spell include Cedric Diggory and Draco Malfoy.

The word Emancipare comes from the Latin phrase ēmancipō, which means to "I set free", it means the same thing in English. Hand movement, Point at the bindings with the wand.

8.Reinnervate (RENN-a-vate): *to revive a victim*

Also known as the counter spell to the stunning spell. The enervate spell is used to restore anyone who has been stunned by a spell.

Effects

The spell comes with a distinctive bright red flash from the caster's wand onto the target. It is also useful in reversing spells from extreme dark spells such as the drink of despair. To cast the spell simply point the wand at the chest of the target.

9.Reparifarge (reh-PAR-i-farj): *Reverses the Effects of an incomplete Transformation spell*

Ron Wesley would be happy to learn the mouse he incompletely transfigured at the Vera verto class can return back to its normal state. The Reparifarge incantation is used to return transfigured animals back to their animal forms. The wizarding world put into consideration that young practising students of the transfiguration magic are bound to get the spell all wrong, thereby resulting in incomplete transfiguration. Thus the need to create a counter-spell such as the Preparifarge.

Taught by Head of the Transfiguration studies department Professor Minerva McGonagall the spell is taught during the second year at Hogwarts. The incantation is culled from the Latin word 'reparo" and "farge" which means to "repair" and "shape" respectively.

Effects

The counterspell gives off a white light when cast.

Section V Jinxes

A jinx is an annoying yet amusing dark spell cast on a target. Their Effects are not as severe as an actual spell or curse. Most jinxes in the wizarding world were created by Severus snape, tom riddle and Merwyn the malicious.

Most Jinxes can be countered using a counter-spell or counter jinx. To prevent being Jinxed an anti-jinx can be used by the target. Sometimes, they are used as a defence against the dark arts. Hence students are thought some jinxes such as the impediment jinx and the Knockback jinx.

1.Oppugno: causes to attack the target.

The oppugno is a Jinx spell that causes commotion in the form of objects attacking a target. This jinx conjures up creatures or other objects against the intended target.

2.Orbis: sucks the target into the ground.

A form of earth magic, used in sucking victims into the ground. It can only work if the target is levitated at the point the spell is cast. It encases the target in an orb and drags them into the earth.

3.Relashio (ruh-LASH-ee-oh): causes the target to drop whatever object he or she is holding.

A compulsive jinx that forces the target to relinquish whatever they are holding. It works on both living and non-living things. It lets off a purple spark and if inside water, the spell fires a jet of boiling water on target and what it's holding.

4.Ventus: shoots a strong blast of wind from the tip of the caster's wand.

Creates a high magnitude cyclone capable of blowing target away. This furious cyclone is controlled from the tips of the caster's wand. Ventus Duo and Ventus Tria are stronger versions of this jinx, creating far more violent gusts of wind. It gives off a grey light when cast.

Section VI Hexes

Hex is a moderate effect dark charm, aimed at inflicting suffering on a target. Hexes are slightly worse than jinxes but are not as dark as curses.

Hexes are used as defense strategy in magical duels. They can also be deflected with either a hex-deflation, hex zapper or a hex-breaker.

Mutatio Skullus (myoo-TAY-toh SKUHL-us): *mutates the target (e.g., target grows extra heads).*

It is the incantation of a hex used to grow a person's head beyond size.

Steleus (STÉ-lee-us): *causes the target to sneeze violently for a short while.*

Causes a victim to sneeze uncontrollably when under the spell.

Titilando (ti-tee-LAN-do): *tickles and weakens the target*

Tickles and weakens the victim. It gives off a purple light when cast as the spell itself resembles purple hands that tickle the target.

Section VII Curses

A curse is a dark charm typical to the worst kinds of dark magic. Primarily defined as any spell that affects the object in a negative manner. While curses come in many strengths and forms, they are generally the strongest, longest-lasting, and least reversible of the Dark charms. The Unforgivable Curses are the strongest known Dark charms in existence, as their Effects are potent and their use requires skill. They are the three most powerful spells in the wizarding world. The three curses are called "unforgivable" because their use has carried the strictest of penalties.

Reducto (re-DUCK-toh): *breaks objects.*

The Reductor Curse is a curse that blasts solid objects to pieces. It is rather easy to reduce a target to a fine mist or a pile of ashes. Harry Potter taught this curse to Dumbledore's Army during the first wizarding war.

Petrificus Totalus (pe-TRI-fi-cus to-TAH-lus): *(Full Body-Bind Curse or Body-Freezing Spell): paralyses the target.*

When used on a living subject, the victim's arms and legs snap together, and they will fall down, stiff as a board. However the person's abilities to hear, see (however just straight forward), feel, and think still work correctly. Hermoine used this spell to petrify Longbottom when he caught sneaking out of bed in ungodly hours during the dreadful times in chambers of secrets.

Sectumsempra: *causes gashes on the target, as if he or she was slashed with an invisible sword.*

Invented by Severus Snape, the curse lacerates and curses severe bleeding on a target. He created it during his childhood, when he was known as "The Half-Blood Prince.harry cast this spell against Malfoy during their duel in the girl's bathroom.

Unbreakable Vow: *Causes a vow that is taken between two witches or wizards to be unbreakable. If one does break the vow, he or she dies.*

An Unbreakable Vow is a magical spell of unknown incantation, in which one witch or wizard makes an oath to another. If either of the two breaks their terms, they die. Bellatrix Lestrange cast this spell between snape and Malfoy's mother to prevent snape from derailing on his promise to protect Malfoy against harm and seeing through that the dark lord's wishes of killing Dumbledore were fulfilled.

Section VIII The Forbidden Section (Unforgivable Curses)

1.Avada Kedavra (Killing Curse) /əˈvɑːdə kəˈdɑːvrə/ ə-vah-də kə-dah-vrə **The Unforgivable Curse;** *Kills your opponent; taken from "Abra Cadabra."*

One of the three unforgivable curses, the Avada Kedavra is the dreadful killing curse often used by the Dark Lord and death eaters to cause instant, painless death to whomever the curse is intended. One of the most potent tools for dark arts, the unforgivable curses are such that no other counter curse or block can prevent part of or the full course of its effect.

The only counter action to prevent the effect of the killing curse is sacrificial protection, born out of pure love. Little wonder why poor harry was saved when his dear mother took the hit of the killing curse from the dark lord.

2.Crucio (KROO-see-oh): *The Second Unforgivable Curse, the Cruciatus Curse; Tortures your opponent mercilessly*

The second unforgivable curse. The cruciatus curse is also known as the torture curse. When cast successfully, the curse inflicts intense, excruciating pain on the victim. A life sentence to Azkaban is the penalty for using any of this three spell including the cruciatus. Once cast, no spell can defend against the Cruciatus Curse. Mad eye moody demonstrated this spell on a tarantula while teaching the

unforgivable curses.

3.Imperio *The third unforgivable curse. Allows the user to assume complete control of another person*

The last and most subtle of the unforgivable curses. To a great extent, the curse can be defended unlike the other two. When cast, the curse places the victim under the caster's complete control. When wrongly cast, the victim's mind would be addled forever. Resisting the Imperius Curse is possible, but requires great strength of will and character, the only unique factor it has among the three.

Chapter Two
Harry Potter Facts
And Trivia

What really do you know about the harry potter franchise aside's obvious. There are many hidden details in the story, and even a magical eye could not spot these. Through the help of our most trusted clairvoyants, we have unrivalled the mystery's behind harry potter, the villain Voldemort, some characters, scenes, and the writer.

1.Jk Rowling Shares The Same Birthdays With Harry Potter.

Not many fans know, the wizarding hero Harry potter shares the same birthdays as JK Rowling the writer, July 31. Another striking similarity, aside sharing birthdays together. Both Harry and Rowling also share the experience of losing their mothers. Rowling told Oprah Winfrey in an interview, "If she hadn't died, I don't think it's too strong to say that there wouldn't be Harry Potter".

2.The Evil Creatures Dementors Were Inspired By Jk Rowling's Struggle With Depression Of Her Mother's Death

The term Dementors was actually born out of the Author's tribulations, fears and depression when her mother died. She has been open about her own struggle with depression when she was in her twenties, saying she was suicidal during that time, similar to the aftereffect of getting attacked by a Dementor. However, the A ray of light and hope (The Patronus spell) is all one needs to overcome the dementors, in her case good memories of the past.

3.The Four Hogwarts Houses Were Invented On a Barf Bag

Gryffindor, Hufflepuff, Slytherin, and Ravenclaw were first written on the back of an aeroplane sick bag when J.K. Rowling was on a plane and didn't want to forget the names before she landed.

4.Before The Word "Quidditch" Was Invented, She Exhausted Fix Notebooks Searching For The Perfect Word

J.K Rowling herself confessed the word Quidditch was decided upon after exhausting five notebooks. JK Rowling said she designed the game in a Manchester hotel room after rowing with her then-boyfriend.

5.Her Initial Idea For The Harry Potter And Philosopher's Stone Was 'Harry Potter And The School Of Magic.'

We all love the ideas behind the Philosopher's stone and Nicolas Flamel, but before J.K Rowling came up with the title we all love and adore today, the original title was harry potter and the school of magic. The reconsideration came afterthought of splitting the story into different books, hence the philosopher's stone.

6.The Final Apart "Deathly Hallows" Were Among The First Parts She Wrote

Many don't know this fact, but the end had already been decided way before the world got to know about Harry Potter. She confessed to having written the first chapters of deathly hallows and carefully hidden it while working on the parts of the book.

7.The Plants Named In The Book Are Culled From a Real Wizarding Book.

In an interview, J.K Rowling confessed, "I used to collect names of plants that sounded witchy and then I found this, Culpeper's Complete Herbal, and it was the answer to my every prayer: flax weed, toadflax, fleawort, Gout-wort, grommel, knotgrass, Mugwort."Nicolas Culpeper was a 17th-century botanist and herbalist who wrote a book on some rear magical plants.

8.Arthur Weasley Was Supposed To Die

J.K Rowling confessed she almost killed off Ron's dad in the order of phoenix when he attacked Voldemort's pet anaconda Nagini because let's face it what's a wizarding tale without a couple of painful deaths. However, she had a second thought considering there wasn't much good father figure in the book. She, however, killed off the characters of Remus Lupin and Nymphadora Tonks, two lovable character's she knew the fans would miss.

9.The Actor Who Played Harry Potter Wasn't The Initial Choice

In the movie adaptation, who would have thought Daniel Radcliff wasn't the first choice, yeah most stars are just that way. The initial choice was Haley Joel Osment; however, things didn't fall through, and after a long time of auditions our harry as we know him was chosen.

10.Dumbledore Was Gay

Who knew the most powerful wizard and headmaster of Hogwarts School of Witchcraft and wizardry was Gay. In 2007, when asked by a fan whether or not Hogwarts's favourite headmaster had ever been in love, Rowling responded, "I always thought of Dumbledore as gay." She revealed that he had fallen in love with Grindelwald, "and that added to his horror when Grindelwald showed himself to be what he was."

11.Moaning Myrtle Was Born Of a Weird Inspiration

Ever thought about how ladies' bathrooms always have a girl crying or sobbing. It could be a bad breakup or a fight with a friend, but there's always a girl crying in some bathroom at some party everyday unlike in boy's bathrooms. Well, that's where she got that inspiration from. And she confessed it she enjoyed placing Harry and Ron in such uncomfortable and unfamiliar territory in Harry Potter and the Chamber of Secrets and Harry Potter and the Half-Blood Prince.

12.Muggles Can't Make Potions

Potions making isn't just about throwing herbs into a boiling pot, a wand is also involved, and like we all know, muggles can't cast a spell even if they said the incantations right. So, for a muggle making a potion, it will just be a pot of really badly made, toxic soup.

13.Dolores Umbridge Was Jailed For Her Cruel Deeds

Miss 'goody two shoes' and lady in Pink Dolores Umbridge did not go scot-free after all she put student's through during her time at Hogwarts. In an interview J.K. Rowling confirmed that Umbridge did indeed get imprisoned for her actions at the Ministry of Magic.

14.Mcgonagall's Animagus Has a Funny Name

We all know the clever witch loves to transform into a cat whenever she pleases. Well, the cat is often called Mrs P. Head.

15.Hagrid Was Never Going To Die

Despite all death scenes and possible dangers the games master experienced, the cheery mini-giant represented the first real father figure in Harry's life; hence his character was plotted to stay and see him through his journey. For this reason also, the author pictured him carrying a 'dead' Harry during the final Hogwarts battle before she had even written Deathly Hallows. This was intended to mirror Hagrid bringing Harry into the wizarding world in the first place in Philosopher's Stone. He was always meant to be there for harry.

16.The Author Once Contemplated Killing Ron

J.K Rowling confessed that during the darkest periods of

her life and writing the book she once contemplated killing of at least one member of the golden trio Ron as the case may be. However, after due considerations, she decided against it. A decision she would always be grateful for.

17.No Muggle Can See Hogwarts The Way It Is

To an average muggle, the Hogwarts school of witchcraft and wizardry is just another dilapidated building in an inhabited forest with a "Keep out: Dangerous" sign on it.

18.Ron And Hermione's Relationship Was a Mistake

The author always regretted the relationship, which eventually led to their marriage. In an interview she admitted it would have suited better between Harry and Hermione which was why she created the tent scene in Half-blood prince, to see the possibility of a romance.

19.The Actual Day The Trio Became Friends

Not the on their way to Hogwarts, not the chocolate from incident nor the sorting hat bonding no. The trio actually became friends on 31st October 2001, when Harry and Ron saved Hermione from the troll in the bathroom. Incidentally this day also was the 10th anniversary of Harry's parent's death, and the first time Voldemort was defeated.

20.Sirius Black And Fred Weasley Both Died Laughing

Both of them were tricksters though, from different generations, both died fighting against Voldemort, both died smiling.

21.Rowling's Years Of Setting The Rules

The first five years Rowling spent on Harry Potter were spent determining rules about what her characters could and could not do.

22. The Greatest Inspiration Behind The Book Was Her Mother's Death

J.K Rowling had said, the Harry Potter books might not have come to fruition if her mother hadn't died. "The books are what they are because she died … because I loved her and she died."

23. Harry's Eye Isn't Always Green In The Movies

In the movie adaptation, J.K Rowling had to admit that not every stuck to the scripts, one of which is the colour of Harry's eye.

24. The Trio Did Their Actual Schoolwork

At any time Harry, Hermione and Ron were seen in class it was actually their real schoolwork, the directors thought this made the scenes look even more real as well as give the kids opportunity to combine acting and schooling.

25. Where Is The Actual Restricted Library Located

The Restricted Section scene was filmed in the Duke Humphrey's building at the Bodleian Library in Oxford. They have very strict rules about not bringing flames into the library. The Harry Potter, motion picture team, was the first-ever to be allowed to break this rule in hundreds of years.

26. What Is The Elder Wand Made Of

We all know Dumbledore's wand is a very powerful old wand, but unlike other wands, the book never made mention of what it was made of. When J.K Rowling was asked about this in an interview, she admitted that the elder wand is made from an ancient magical tree known as the 'death tree'. Also Dumbledore, who could perform magic without needing to say the incantation aloud, using ˜homenum revelio'.

27.All Names Have Been Intricately Selected To Reflect Their Roles

J.K Rowling without doubts, has the strong word-building ability ever seen in modern literary fictions sphere. The names of her characters embody the role of the character. Even before she started the first chapter, the names of the 40 Hogwarts students in Harry's year were already known.

28.No One Noticed The English Translation Of The Hogwarts Motto

The Hogwarts motto which like most potter terms is written in Latin, "Draco dormiens nunquam titillandus", unlike most school mottos which could stand for nobility, fidelity, clarity or perseverance, the motto means "Never tickle a sleeping dragon". We promise never to anyway.

29.The "Harry Potter" Books Have Been Translated Into Around 80 Languages.

From Albanian to Hebrew to Scots, and collectively selling over 500 million copies worldwide.

30.What Happened To Peeves In The Movie

One of the prominent supernatural characters in the book was peeves the Hogwarts ghost. However, in the movie adaptation, no one saw peeves. Many who didn't read the book don't even know about peeves existence.

31.The Brooms Used In The Series Aren't Regular

In case you thought these were the regular fibre brooms your grandma locks up in a top-shelf sorry co they're not. The actual material as divulged by the production crew is aeroplane-grade titanium. The reason, the kids had to sit on them while the props create the flying scenes, you don't want little harry breaking an arm for real.

32.The Actual Actor Who Paly Ron Has a Real Fear For Spiders

Rupert Grint has an actual severe case of arachnophobia. This made it very easy to fl the scene as he portrayed a natural reaction to seeing the spider.

33.Nymphadora's Hair Deviated From The Books

Going by the scripts, Miss Tonks was actually described as bubblegummy pink. However, the directors decide the colour should be purely associated with Umbridge. Hence tonks settled for a purple hair.

34.Blood Ties

The actor who played young Tom riddle is actually related to Voldemort. He is hero Fiennes-tiffin, a nephew to Lord Voldemort Ralph Fiennes. Also Bill Weasley and Mad-Eye Moody have an intimate connection. Domhnall Gleeson portrays Bill Weasley and is the son of Brendan Gleeson, who plays Mad-Eye Moody. Can you spot the resemblance?

35.Harry And Ron Never Graduated From Hogwarts

As surprising as it may sound the almighty harry potter is a school drop-out alongside his friend Ron Weasley, but who needs a piece of paper to prove you're the bravest wizards of their age. After all, to take down Voldemort is not an easy task.

After Voldemort was killed, the duo declined to finish their education at Hogwarts. Harry and Ron became Aurors (those who fight against dark wizards). Hermione, on the other hand, got a job at the department of magical law enforcement. Eventual the smart witch rose to the position of the minister of magic.

36.The Trio Was Featured On The Chocolate Frog Cards

According to J.K. Rowling, Ron's most beautiful moment was when he saw his own portrait on a Chocolate Frog Card. Harry, Ron, and Hermione deserved such an honour for their impact in the overthrowing of Voldemort's regime.

37.How Old Were Voldemort And Dumbledore When They Died

Dumbledore died at a very old and ripe age of: 115 years old. Voldemort died at the age of 71 after he failed woefully to make himself immortal.

38.Moaning Myrtle Was No Teenager

Aside from her strange voice and innocent demeanour, she is one tough lady to play this part. According to the story, moaning myrtle died in the girl's bathroom at the age of 14. However Shirley Henderson the actress who played this part was actually 36 when she acted the part in chambers of secrets.

39.Hagrid Was Never Able To Cast a Patronus

Our favourite game master was never able to cast one of the most powerful and difficult spells known in the wizarding world. Good thing he never got in contact with dementors either.

40.Hogwarts Is a Tuition-Free School.

Well, we can only thank the ministry of magic for the immeasurable benevolence. JK Rowling disclosed this surprising revelation to potter fans during an interview. Stating that the ministry takes care of all school expenses.

41.Wizards Under The Age Of 11 Have To Study At Home.

All children under the age of eleven according to a decree passed by the international statute of secrecy must not practice magic openly without the supervision of an adult, in this case, a home tutor. They are considered minors and unable to control their magical powers thus susceptible to revealing themselves to ordinary people.

42.The Phoenix Is The Author's Favourite Mythical Creature

Long before she wrote the books, J.K Rowling always has

a soft spot for this legendary mythical bird and al the stories associated with it. According to Rowling, the reason why the bird intrigues her is because phoenixes can live up to 1000 years and this is possible because they burst into flames and rise from the ashes again, 'reborn' when they are ill or sick. Secondly, their tears have healing powers capable of healing wounds. Lastly, they are incredibly loyal creatures.

When Dumbledore died, Fawkes, too, left Hogwarts for good. Rowling said, "Dumbledore was a very great and irreplaceable man, and the loss of Fawkes (and the fact that he was 'non-transferable'!) Expresses this symbolically." Thus portraying the loyalty of the bird to its owner.

43.What Does Dumbledore Often Dream About?

One can only imagine what a powerful old wizard would dream about when he wanders off to dreamland. Dumbledore's most famous dream is his family reunion. The mirror of Erised which shows a person's deepest wishes and dreams revealed this. In it, Dumbledore saw a family reunion with his father, mother, and sister all alive, happy and together. His brother too was kinder to him in this dream. Hence, harry was tricked with the wool socks stuff he told him about.

44.Dean Thomas Always Thought He Was Muggle-Born

The young wizard was unaware of his magical backgrounds due to the absence of his biological father from his life while he was growing up. Hence, Dean Thomas grew up with the assumption that he was a muggle-born.

45.The Real Meaning Behind Molly Weasley Killing Bellatrix Lestrange

Many wonder how possible it was for an average housewife and mother to many children to kill a powerful dark witch and closest ally to Lord Voldemort Bellatrix Lestrange. A witch responsible for the deaths of many good wizards and wildly twisted by her love for her master. Why molly? An apparent symbol of lesser magical strength due to her role in the book. Because she represents motherly love and protection: the values that should always win.

46. What Are The Original Names Of The Characters?

These were some of the original names of the characters before Rowling changed them: Hermione Puckle, Neville Puff, Draco Spinks, Lily Moon (Luna Lovegood), Madhari Patil, and Mati Patil.

47. The Weasley Twins Fred And George Were Born On April Fool's Day

Well, that explains a lot of things. Doesn't it?

48. Remus Lupin Hated All Things Wolf

For a wizard who is a werewolf, isn't this a rather awkward hatred. For this reason, his patronus is a wolf rather than a werewolf.

49. Love Can Change a Patronus

A patronus often comes as a representation of a wizard's nature but in an animal form. Severus love for Harry's mother made his patronus change to a doe after she died. Nymphadora Tonks' original Patronus was a jackrabbit, but it eventually changed to a wolf. Remus was killed by Antonin Dolohov, and Tonks was killed by Bellatrix Lestrange.

50. What Do We Really Know About Professor Mcgonagall?

Who knew professor McGonagall was very good at quidditch. Minerva McGonagall was an excellent player during her time at Hogwarts. However a severe accident in her final year leaving her with a broken rib and concussion derailed her from ever playing the game again.

She fell in love with a young muggle boy shortly after her graduation who proposed to her, and although she loved him she couldn't accept in fear of revealing her true identity unless they had kids. Breaking this law was in violation of the International Statute of Secrecy, she would lose the job at the Ministry thus she gave him up.

Shortly after this heartbreak, Minerva left for London and took up a teaching post at Hogwarts. She eventually married her old boss Elphinstone Urquart after several persuasion. Unfortunately, he dies three years into the marriage after a venomous tarantula bite.

51.What Happened To The Death Eater's After Voldemort's Death

The Death Eaters' Dark Marks eventually faded into scars. They no longer burn or hurt. The ministry arrested some of them and jailed them to Azkaban, the lucky escapees went into hiding and were never seen after.

52.Deathly Hallows Was Based On The Pardoner's Tale By Geoffrey Chaucer.

J.K Rowling disclosed that she drew the most inspiration for deathly hallows from the book The Pardoner's Tale by Geoffrey Chaucer.

53.Harry And Voldemort's Relationship

Aside from their magical ties, Harry potter is related to Voldemort by blood. Surprised? Nearly all wizarding families are related if you trace them back through the centuries. As was made evident in ˜Deathly hallows', Peverell blood would run through many wizarding families.

54.Hedwig Died For a Reason

Harry's pet Hedwig was very dear to the young wizard. The author killed Hedwig to signify the loss of innocence and security, her death marked the end of Harry's childhood.

55.Dumbledore Was The Only One Who Could See Harry Under His Invisibility Cloak

Although young harry never knew this fact. Dumbledore silently cast the human-presence-revealing spell, homenum revelio, to detect Harry under his invisibility cloak.

56.What Happened To The Dementors?

After Voldemort was defeated, the ministry regulated so many aspects of the wizarding world, one of which was the presence of dementors as guards in Azkaban. When Kingsley Shacklebolt was made the permanent head of the Ministry of Magic, he banned the use of Dementors to guard Azkaban, and everywhere else in the wizarding world.

57.What Magical Power Does The Author Crave For?

Rowling confessed that she would love to have the power of invisibility. When asked why she answered, "If I had any power, I would have the power of invisibility, and this is a little bit sad, but I would probably sneak off to a café and write all day."

58.Ginny Was Always Meant For Harry

Irrespective of what we all hoped for, an obvious harry and Hermione romance. J.K Rowling had been secretly plotting Ginny Weasley for harry longer than we imagined. An evident moment was when Ginny beat choc hang in quidditch.

59.The Character Hermione Was Based Off j.k Rowling Herself

Hermione is a mirror image of who Rowling was at a tender age. An avid reader who as curious about all things. Even her patronus an otter is Rowling's favourite animal.

Chapter Three-
Fantastic
Beasts

A comprehensive lists of all the magical creatures/ ghosts, animals and ghouls in the harry potter franchise.

- Acromantula
- Basilisk
- Boggarts
- Centaurs
- Dementors
- Devil's Snare
- Dragon
- Ghosts
- Giants
- Goblins
- Hippogriff
- House-Elves
- Merperson
- Mountain Troll
- Obscurials/Obscurus
- Owls
- Owls
- Pixie
- Thestrals
- Three-Headed Dogs
- Unicorns
- Werewolves

Acromantula

Acromantulas are fierce-looking flesh-eating spiders that live in dense jungles and forested areas. They are gigantic creatures that originate from Borneo, having legs that measure up to fifteen feet each. One of their distinguishing features is the thick black hair that covers most parts of their body.

Acromantulas are dangerous and dreaded for their deadly

venom, which they secrete on prey. They often set traps using dome-shaped webs to catch prey. Some of them are capable of human speech if they stay for a long time with humans.

The first appearance of an Acromantula was in Harry Potter and the Chamber of Secrets. The most popular of them was Aragog, who was raised by Rubeus Hagrid, the gamekeeper at Hogwarts School of Witchcraft and Wizardry.

He had an Acromantula wife named, Mosag. Aragog was thought to be the monster in the Chamber of Secrets. Ron and Harry came face to face with him when Aragog's children captured them in the Forbidden Forest and led them to their father.

Harry later discovered that Aragog was wrongly accused of being the wasn't the monster. They eventually became friends until Aragog died of an unknown illness on April 20, 1997.

Basilisk

A Basilisk is what you would call an anaconda version of Medusa. It is a light green monstrous snake that spreads death with either its huge yellow eyes or its lethal venom. It's likened to Medusa because all it takes to kill any living creature is one look into its eyes. However, when one looks at it through reflections or when ghosts look at it directly, they'll get petrified.

Typically, a Basilisk can grow up to about fifty feet in length and can live for many centuries. Unlike most creatures, the only people who can control them are Parselmouths. Parselmouths are people who can speak the language of snakes, Parseltongue. Stories have it that a notable Greek Dark Wizard and Parelmouth, Herpo The Foul, created the first Basilisk.

After wrongly accusing Aragog the Acromantula of being the monster in the Chamber of Secrets, it was later discovered that a female Basilisk was indeed the fearsome creature responsible for the death of a girl, Moaning Myrtle (whose full name is Myrtle Elizabeth Warren) in 1943.

Everyone knew the basilisk as the Serpent of Slytherin. She earned her name after Salazar Slytherin, the wizard who placed her in the Chamber of Secrets. She could only be controlled by Tom Riddle, the heir of Slytherin, who later became Lord Voldermort. This means that other Parselmouths, including

Harry Potter, could only understand but had zero control over her.

The Serpent of Slytherin eventually met her death at the hands of Harry Potter, who was helped by Fawkes, Dumbledore's phoenix. Fawkes blinded the basilisk's eyes with his talons, thereby giving Harry Potter a fighting chance against the petrifying snake. Harry wielded the sword of Godric Gryffindor and drove it into the roof of the Basilisk's mouth, killing her.

Boggarts

Not many creatures can be described as "amortal." Boggarts happen to be one of them because they were never born and cannot die either. A Boggart is a shape-shifter that can assume the form of its victim's deepest fears. They originate from Scotland and can cause untold misery.

No one can expressly tell what a boggart looks like when it hasn't taken the form of its victim's fear. However, its shape-shifting feature makes it somewhat easy for someone with a magical eye to discover its presence.

Without being seen, notable evidence of its presence is shaking and scratching of the object it's occupying. The perfect place to find Boggarts are in dark, enclosed areas like cabinets. In Harry Potter and the Order of the Phoenix, Alastor Moody was able to discover one hiding in a desk at the Headquarters of the Order.

Boggarts were common in Harry Potter and the Prisoner of Azkaban. In different instances, Remus Lupin taught his students how to defend themselves against creatures of dark magic, such as boggarts. They were able to use the Riddikulus charm to fight against Boggarts by changing the appearance of the creatures to something less scary than the potential victims' worst fear.

For Harry Potter, his deepest fear has always been Dementors. As such, when he approached a Boggart, it took the form of a dementor.

Centaurs

Centaurs are highly intelligent creatures with significant semblance with humans. A centaur is a half-horse, half-human. From head to torso, it has the full physical attributes of humans, but the abdomen to toes are those of a horse with a complementing tail.

Despite their resemblance to humans, centaurs are known to dissociate themselves from human affairs and civilization. They live in forests in colonies or herds. Their weapons of war for all centuries have comprised mainly of bows of arrows with no desire to borrow the sophistication of humans.

However, in Harry Potter and the Philosopher's Stone, Harry met Firenze, a centaur who doesn't share the same philosophy with his kind as regards association with humans. First, he saved Harry from death on the Forbidden Forest and then carried him (Harry) on his back to safety. It was an action that other Centaurs considered to be derogatory and spiteful.

Firenze eventually got a job to teach Divination at Hogwarts. Unfortunately, his soft spot for humans led to his banishment from his Centaur herd. He was subsequently attacked and almost killed by his people, if not for the timely intervention of Rubeus Hagrid.

Centaurs' relationship with humans took a different shape in Harry Potter and the Deathly Hollows. Hagrid successfully mobilized and admonished the Hogwarts centaur herd and had them side with the Order of the Phoenix during the Battle of Hogwarts.

Dementors

Dementors are popular for being Harry Potter's most feared creatures. They are soulless beings with the ability to rid humans of their emotions and intelligence, replacing them with fear and depression. They appear to have human-like figures, measuring about ten meters in height.

But they are always seen with dark, hooded cloaks revealing only their shriveled hands. Beneath their cloaks, Dementors have no eyes. Nonetheless, they can sense the presence and movement of humans and other beings. One of their greatest weapons is their indrawn breath with which they steal the pleasant memories of humans.

Up until the invasion of Voldermort, Dementors were the guards of Azkaban, the wizard prison. This alliance between the Ministry of Magic and Dementors to keep watch over Azkaban was much frowned at by Albus Dumbledore, who believes Dementors are exceedingly vile creatures who shouldn't have anything to do with the rest of the magical worlds.

He banned them from entering Hogwarts, and the ban was effective until the Minister of Magic, Cornelius Fudge, broke it in Harry Potter and the Prisoner of Azkaban. Fudge insisted he wanted a Dementor as a bodyguard and successfully had his way.

They grow in dark, moist places like fungi, and a cold and dark feeling characterizes their presence. One of Harry's notable encounters with dementors was in Harry Potter and the Prisoner of Azkaban when he and some students were sent to guard Hogwarts against Sirius Black, who was thought to be a dangerous criminal.

In the Order of the Phoenix, Harry survived an assassination attempt at the hands of two Dementors sent by Minister Fudge's secretary, Dolores Umbridge. In the later part of the book, the Dementors guarding Azkaban revolted against the Ministry of Magic, taking sides with Voldemort. They were also used by Voldermont-controlled Ministry in the Deathly Hallows to punish Muggle-borns.

Devil's Snare

Devil's Snare is one of those plants that shouldn't be admired. It's a magical plant with the ability to constrict and swallow up anything that comes close to it. It's considered a fantastic beast due to its sentient nature. As it is with some other creatures, the Devil's Snare is very rare and is accessible to only a few herbologists.

It has soft, springy tendrils and vines that possess some sense of touch. It uses its tendrils and vines to trap any living thing that touches it. It goes ahead to bound their arms and legs tightly and in the process choke them to death

Struggling with the grasp of Devil's Snare causes it to constrict even harder, leading to death. Since it's sensitive to motion, a practical way of freeing one's self from its grip is to remain still until the plant stops recording any movement around it, making it drop its captive.

Due to its preference for dark and damp environments, Devil's snare doesn't thrive well in front of bright light. It will also be seen recoiling whenever the heat of fire comes close. And so, to drive it away from its victims, a flame or light-based spells such as a fire-making spell, bluebell flames, Lumos Solem spell, or wand-lighting charm or Lumos Solem spell can be cast.

In Harry Potter and the Philosopher's Stone, Harry, Ron, and Hermione got trapped in the Devil's Snare's grip while they were trying to prevent the Philosopher's Stone from being. Hermione was able to free herself quickly enough from the grasp of the plant, while Harry and Ron were stuck and had started to suffocate. Hermione set the plant on fire using the Bluebell Flames spell and freed her friends.

Dragon

These snorting reptiles are famed for their humongous wings and fire breathing abilities. Their ultra-normal fire breathing skills are not limited to their mouths as they can also expel their explosive missiles through their nostrils.

They have giant wings and very thick skins. While they are almost impossible to domesticate, Dragon Keepers or Dragonologists are known to possess the rare gift of communicating and training dragons. Rubeus Hagrid so much loved dragons that he briefly owned a Norwegian Ridgeback dragon named Norbert in Harry Potter and the Philosopher's Stone.

Harry, Hermione, and Ron were there when Norbert was hatched. Harry also faced a Hungarian Horntail Dragon in the Goblet of Fire when he had to retrieve the golden egg in a task.

Ghosts

Ghosts are silvery and translucent looking beings who are the souls of dead wizards and witches. Not all dead wizards and witches are ghosts. It is a decision they have to make, whether to travel to the world beyond or to stay back as ghosts.

Unlike the popular concept, ghosts in Harry Potter books aren't necessarily scary. They can interact freely with humans and can leverage their experience to play advisory roles to the living. In the Ministry of Magic, they have full legal rights and operate under the "Spirit Division."

Ghosts can fly and have the rare ability to walk through objects and walls. Some of them, like Moaning Myrtle, can touch and feel physical things. Every house in Hogwarts has a ghost. They include Nearly Headless Nick, whose real name was Sir Nicholas De Mimsy-Porpington, the Bloody Baron, the Fat Friar, and the Grey Lady who was killed by the Bloody Baron.

Another famous ghost is Professor Binns, who is a professor of history at Hogwarts. He died in his sleep and woke up as a ghost, only to resume his lectures the next day. Harry had a conversation with Nearly Headless Nick in Harry Potter and the Order of the Phoenix, where he explained to Harry his fear about traveling to the world beyond.

Giants

Giants don't need much introduction as they are famous creatures in European folklore. They are exceedingly tall creatures measuring between twenty to twenty-five feet in height. However, there are some of them like Grawp in the Order of the Phoenix, who has a seemingly low height of only sixteen feet.

Giants have mainly been hunted by wizards, which led to their alienation from humans. As a result, they are only a very few of them left. They live in a confined region of Britain known as Belarus. Some of them who have survived the onslaught of the ferocious wizardry attacks have their rhinoceros-like skin to thank. The skin gives them some level of immunity against magical attacks.

The Gurgs loosely govern their activities as a species. It's easy to identify Gurgs as the largest, laziest, and ugliest giants in a tribe. They spend their days eating the foods from their subordinates. Some giants are half-breeds such as Rubeus Hagrid and his love, Olympe Maxime.

Hagrid and Maxime once went to the Giants to convince them to join forces with the Ministry of Magic against Voldermort. But the negotiations failed when Golgomath executed an assassination on the Gurg. Upon his death, the giants took side with Voldermort in the Battle of Hogwarts, who promised them a better life.

Goblins

Goblins are small magical humanoids or anthropoids with characteristic features that resemble house-elves. They have long, fingers, and feet. Some of them have noses that are nearly as long as Pinocchio's. They also have significantly long ears and domed shaped heads that are quite large in proportion to the body size.

They are skilled metalsmiths and renowned for their mastery over silverworks. Goblins are in charge of the Gringotts bank, which is the only mentioned bank in the wizardry world. As part of their duties, they mint coins for the bank and have a significant dominance over the wizardry economy.

Goblins communicate in a language known simply as Gobbledegook. They can be said to be carnivorous since they feast on raw meat. But they also eat roots and fungi. Their relationship with wizards has been fraught for hundreds of years and has often led to violence. As such, wizarding law makes it a crime for goblins to own wands. However, goblins have their magic that does not need a wand to use it.

They've existed as far back as the time of Godric Gryffindor, but due to their strained relationship with wizards, they are treated as second-class citizens. They decided not to take sides during the Second Wizarding War between the Ministry and Voldemort. Bill Weasley is one of the few goblins with certain levels of friendship with wizards. He works as a Curse Breaker for Gringotts banks.

Griphook is probably one of the most popular goblins. In Harry Potter and the Deathly Hallows, he assisted Harry and his friends to find the Helga Hufflepuff's Cup and played his role towards the defeat of Lord Voldermort.

Hippogriff

A hippogriff is a fierce-looking magical creature having the form of both an eagle and a horse. It has large orange eyes and a sharp steel-colored beak. Its front legs, wings, and head take the form of a giant eagle, while the body, hind legs, and tail are fashioned like that of a horse. The talons on its front legs were half a foot long and dangerously sharp. It is very similar to a Griffin, although it replaces Griffin's lion rear with that of a horse.

Although fierce-looking might be an adequate term for this magical creature, the hippogriff is also an impressive looking creature. Hippogriffs come in different colors, including stormy grey, bronze, pinkish roan, gleaming chestnut, and inky black. It has shiny gleaming coats, which easily transitions from feathers to hair.

Hippogriffs are carnivorous and can be extremely dangerous if not tamed by trained. The hippogriff feeds mainly on worms, insects, birds, and small mammals.

Hippogriffs breeds in a seemingly odd way. They build nests on the ground and lays just one egg, which is very fragile. Their eggs hatch within a record time of twenty-four hours. Infant Hippogriff mature pretty quick, and can fly within a week, though it takes a long while before they are strong enough to go on longer journeys with their parents

Hippogriffs are incredibly proud creatures, and so anyone approaching them must be courteous enough to bow and wait for the creature to reciprocate the bow. Also, eye contact must be maintained at all times without a single blink.

A herd of hippogriffs was kept at Hogwarts. Buckbeak was a part of the Hogwarts herd. He lived with Rubeus Hagrid but was later sentenced to death for attacking Draco Malfoy in Harry Potter and the Prisoner of Azkaban. Harry Potter saved him from the execution, after which he came under the care of Sirius Black. At the death of Sirius, Harry claimed ownership of him.

Although proud, Hippogriffs are also very loyal creatures demonstrated by Buckbeak when he attacked Severus Snape in a bid to defend Harry Potter during the Battle of the Astronomy Tower.

House-Elves

House-elves are two to three feet tall creatures often used by wizards as slaves. They are characterized by slender limbs, oversized eyes, and pretty large heads. Their ears are considerable large also, compared to the size of their bodies. The ears are pointed and look like those of bats.

House-elves speak in squeaky voices and refer to themselves in the third person. It's hard to tell if they have surnames too. They are very obedient and loyal — two qualities that qualify them to serve as slaves to wizards. It's not uncommon to see them wearing tattered clothes. To free an enslaved House-elf, the master will give them a piece of clothing.

However, an enslaved House-elf can still choose to disobey his master if the instructions could affect his friends negatively. Often, a disobedient house-elf would punish itself for being disobedient. As magical creatures, house-elves also have a little magic with which they carry out their masters' instructions. One of their notable magical powers is Teleportation. They can teleport to any place even within Hogwarts and other places where human Teleportation is forbidden.

Besides Teleportation and house chores, House-elves can use some powerful magic, powerful enough to repel wizards. Harry has a long history with them and their constant help. In the Goblet of Fire, Dobby (a house-elf) used its magic to protect Harry against Lucius Malfoy. Kreacher was quite resourceful in Deathly Hallows in capturing Mundungus Fletcher, bringing him to 12 Grimmauld Place for Harry.

Merperson

Merpeople are magical creatures that live in water. Their head to the chest is like humans, while their abdomen and yonder look like a fish. They are quite thin with long arms. Merpeople have a rocky relationship with wizards, refusing to be recognized as "beings." Instead, they chose the status of "beasts."

They live in colonies and have distinct facial appearances. Some members of the Black Lake Merpeople Colony that live on the grounds of Hogwarts Castle have yellow eyes, green hair, and grey skin. Their tails are often silvery, and on an average, a Merperson is taller than a human, measuring up to seven feet from head to tail.

Merpeople have a history that dates back to ancient Greek civilization. They were initially known as Sirens up until the modern era when their kind spread across the world. Although they've been mentioned in earlier books of the series, the first appearance of a Merperson was in Harry Potter and the Goblet of Fire.

Harry encountered one in the Black Lake. He was seven feet tall, had a long green beard, and was willing a spear.

Mountain Troll

The Mountain Troll is the largest breed of trolls. Bald, ogre-like in structure and with the biggest mismatched two-toe feet ever seen, the mountain troll's only piece of clothing is a two-piece brown shawl. One wraps the torso, and the other is worn over like a monkey jacket.

It has large and amorphous ears and a dramatically rotund belly. Its head is too small for its bulky frame, and its hands end in claw-like nails. This brutish beast is about 12 feet, weighs a tonne, and demonstrates a typical stupidity unbecoming of its size.

Its first appearance is in Harry Potter and the Philosopher's Stone when Prof. Quirrell, the teacher of Defence Against the Dark Arts, makes a terrifying announcement at the Halloween feast about a troll in the building.

Harry soon realized that Hermione was unaware of this fact. Alongside Ron, he dashed out to inform her. However, by some act of oversight, their concerted efforts resulted in them locking the troll in the girls' bathroom, leaving Hermione trapped with it.

Poised with determination, each other's support, and a slice of magic from Ron's wand, they were able to win against the troll and save Hermione.

Obscurials/Obscurus

Obscurials are children of magic who so much suppressed their magic that it became a dark force within them known as Obscurus. The major reason behind such suppressions is the persistent hunt of people with magic, thereby ridding them of a sense of belonging in society. Apart from being depressed occasionally, the Obscurial behaves calmly until their power is unleashed when the child is exceedingly distress.

During such incidents, the Obscurus will take over the child's body leaving him with insufficient power to fight back the dark force. The child's eye will turn creamy white as he gets violent against its victim, who must have caused him some distress. The attack is so severe that they leave burn marks on their victims.

Once it's satisfied, the parasitic Obscurus will return freedom to the host Obscurial. Due to their violent nature, the host Obscurials rarely live beyond their childhood. Witches and wizards are afraid of those who grow into adolescent age and are considered people of dark magic. Their uncontrollable outburst of violence is seen as a threat to the International Statute of Secrecy.

Despite Harry's troublesome childhood, he narrowly escaped being an Obscurial. This is because the Dursleys who Harry grew up with didn't acknowledge the existence of magic to him. So the young Harry didn't believe he had magic, and as such, didn't try to suppress it.

Owls

Owls are very common fantastic beasts whose skills are needed for everyday wizard living. They are birds of prey, feeding on insects, worms, and other birds. They live in trees, caves, barns, and others live in the homes if wizards.

Owls are renowned for their wide eyes and strong wings. They have a rare skill that enhances communication in the wizardry world. They can deliver parchments, parcels, letters, and Howlers to any destination. They are magical creatures and can find any witch or wizard without a need for an address.

Their services can be commercialized as it is in the Owl

Post Office in Hogsmeade, Daily Prophet, and The Quibbler. Harry had an owl called Hedwig. She is snowy white and is one of Harry's best buddies featuring in most books of the series, including the Philosopher's Stone. Another notable owl in the series is Errol, which belongs to the Weasley family.

Phoenix

The phoenix is a large magical bird with red and gold-colored plumage. Its crimson feathers have a faint glow in the dark, and its golden peacock-like tail is hot when touched. It is doubtful though whether they do burn as Harry Potter wasn't burnt by the Phoenix's feather tail when Fawkes carried him in the Chamber of Secrets.

The phoenix is immune to the deadly gaze of the Basilisk, whose eye contact with another creature would instantly lead to their death or petrification when looked at through a reflection. The tears of the phoenix are the only known cure to the Basilisk venom.

The tail of the phoenix serves some supernatural purposes for it. It can be used as a carrier of messages when the Phoenix goes up in flames and appears somewhere else only to leave behind a single golden tail feather. The strength of its tail is also overwhelming as it can lift great weight attached to its tail.

They are extremely personal creatures and can demonstrate a human-like level of loyalty and help to beings they care about. For instance, Harry couldn't have slain the Basilisk without the help of Fawkes.

Pixie

These small and intensely mischievous creatures are famous for their pranks, sly jokes and mischief. The pixies are an arresting shade of blue, possess elf-like ears with pink in the enclosures. Their noses are formidably long like Pinocchio's, and this feature, just like every other feature of the pixie's angular face, points to mischief lurking somewhere.

While pixies are usually confused with imps as they share similar height and biting sense of humor, the two differ in that the pixies can fly. The height of the average adult pixie is about eight inches, and its trademark shrill and squeaky voice is only intelligible to its fellow pixies.

The pixie, as part of its roguish exercise, enjoys to lift people by the ears and dump them at the top of trees or buildings, thus displaying an uncanny amount of strength unexpected for creatures of that size. The pixies' notorious mischief also expresses itself in its proclivity to stealing things.

They make their debut appearance in Harry Potter and the Chamber of Secrets when, in 1994, a water well on the ground of Hogwarts School of Witchcraft & Wizardry, became infested with a drone of pixies. It somehow fell on Harry, Ronald Weasely and Hermione Granger to rid out the infestation with the use of tickling charm.

Much later in 1998, at the Battle of Hogwarts, Harry came across these creatures again when he stumbled upon a cage containing cornish pixies in the Room of Requirements while searching for Ravenclaw's diadem.

Thestrals

Thestrals are skeletal, carnivorous winged horses. They are pretty elusive and can be seen only by those who have witnessed death. A first look at it reveals its white eyes, bony body, proud wings, long tail, and dragon-like face. Their skeletal framework is probably not far from the reason that they can only be seen by those who have embraced death.

Beyond appearing scary, Thestrals are relatively gentle. They have fierce fangs which they use on their prey and in battles. Their heightened sense of smell is very resourceful when they need to track flesh blood and carrions.

Despite their wild characteristics, Thestrals can be domesticated and can be a loyal friend at the hands of a diligent trainer. They can take fast, and long flights, an ability Harry leveraged on in the Order of the Phoenix. Hogwarts has a herd of Thestrals in the Forbidden Forest which they use to pull the carriage that transports students to and from the Hogsmeade train station

Harry was able to see these creatures after he witnessed the death of Cedric Diggory. In Harry Potter and the Deathly Hallows, they took sides with the Ministry in the Battle of Hogwarts, fighting against Death Eaters.

Three-Headed Dogs

The Three-Headed Dog is a very rare fantastic beast that was seen only a very few times in the Harry Potter series. It's fierce-looking, possessing great strength and speed. It's probably modeled after Cerberus, the Three-Headed Dog in Greek mythology.

The three heads are coordinated and communicate among themselves. It's just like a regular dog, except for its heads. This creature, despite its fierceness, has a weakness, which is its inability to stay awake when it hears the sound of music.

The only Three-Headed Dog mentioned in the series is Fluffy. His loyalty to Hagrid shows the beast can be domesticated. Hagrid bought it from a Greek man in Hogsmeade. In Harry Potter and the Philosopher's Stone, Hermione, Harry, Ron, and Neville came face to face with Fluffy while trying to avoid Filch.

They later discovered that the beast had been guarding the pathway to the Philosopher's Stone. Carelessly, Hagrid had revealed the weakness of the Three-Headed Dog to Snape, whom he had gotten a dragon's egg from. Using the same musical weakness of Fluffy, Harry and his friends set out to find the Stone before Snape could do so.

Unicorns

Unicorns are white horned horse-like animals. They are transcending creatures, born gold-colored, and gradually change to a silver-tone at the age of four. They turn to pure white color at adulthood.

Their horns and hairs are magical as they can be used for various potions and bandages. Once their blood is taken by anyone at the brink of death, such one would be brought back to life, but at the risk of his living a cursed life. It is the same reason wizards don't use the blood of the Phoenix in potions as the drinker will live a cursed life once he recovers.

Unicorns are regal and majestic, especially at their fully grown stature. Harry Potter's first encounter with one was in Harry Potter & the Philosopher's Stone. He, Hermione, Ron, and Draco were serving their detention with Hagrid in the Forbidden

Forest. They had a task to find a wounded unicorn.

Harry and Draco eventually found it dead beside a hooded man who was drinking its blook. The man tried to harm Harry, but a Centaur, Firenze, was on time to deliver Harry from the hooded man. The Centaur carried Harry away in safety on his back to Hagrid, a move that eventually cost Firenze his relationship with his kind.

Werewolves

A werewolf is a humanoid with the ability to exist as a human and also as a wolf-like creature. Irrespective of the form he takes, he is referred to as a werewolf. Werewolves can only change into their wolf nature during full moons. During such states, they look almost exactly like wolves except for a few distinct features like their claws, eyes, ears, snout, claws, and tufted tail.

The curse of werewolf, which is called Lycanthropy, is not a detestable condition in the wizardry world. It is hereditary but with a few exceptions, such as the case of Teddy Lupin, who comes from a generation of werewolves. A common way of becoming a werewolf is to be bitten by a werewolf while it's in its wolf form.

Werewolves are highly dangerous and feared among witches and wizards primarily because while in their wolf form, they are very animalistic and lack their human mind. This can make them hurt people, including the ones they love. There hasn't been any notable cure for the condition, but the Wolfsbane Potion is renowned for helping them control the Effects of the condition.

For instance, the potion can help a werewolf maintain control of his human mind even while in his wolf form, thereby preventing him from hurting people. However, the potion is exceedingly bitter and scarcely available. Werewolves live far away because the wizards, out of fear, alienated them from the normal society.

Teddy's father, Remus Lupin, is the only known werewolf who didn't align with Voldermort. In Harry Potter and the Half-Blood Prince, others werewolves, such as Fenrir Greyback, partook in The Battle of the Astronomy Tower, fighting alongside the dark lord.

Printed in Great Britain
by Amazon

35256197R00038